Pirates
of the
Storm

by Enid Richemont and Andy Hammond

W
FRANKLIN WATTS
LONDON•SYDNEY

This is a story about Mary Read and Anne Bonny, but these women really were pirates who lived over three hundred years ago. It is said that Mary dressed like a man to set out for a life at sea. The women sailed together and did actually fight when Calico Jack and his crew were too drunk to do so!

First published in 2010 by
Franklin Watts
338 Euston Road
London NW1 3BH

Franklin Watts Australia
Level 17/207 Kent Street
Sydney NSW 2000

Text © Enid Richemont 2010
Illustrations © Andy Hammond 2010

A CIP catalogue record for this book is available
from the British Library.

ISBN 978 0 7496 9440 1 (hbk)
ISBN 978 0 7496 9446 3 (pbk)

Series Editor: Jackie Hamley
Series Advisor: Catherine Glavina
Series Designer: Peter Scoulding

Printed in China

Franklin Watts is a division of
Hachette Children's Books,
an Hachette UK company
www.hachette.co.uk

For Jude and Anna,
with love – E.R.

Long ago, there lived two women called Mary Read and Anne Bonny.

MARY READ   ANNE BONNY

Mary grew up in England. In those days, girls in England weren't allowed adventures …

... so Mary dressed up as a boy and ran away.

Anne grew up across the ocean in America. Like Mary, Anne longed for adventure ...

... so she married a pirate called Calico Jack.

One day, Mary arrived at a port.
"A life at sea looks exciting,"
she thought.

"Anyone need a cabin boy?"
Mary yelled.

A cruel captain grabbed her.

"I do," he growled.

Anne, too, longed to go to sea.
But Calico Jack's crew did not want
her on their ship. "Women bring
bad luck," they growled.

Anne did not give up. One day, she
hid her hair and put on breeches.
"I'm your cabin boy now,"
she told Jack.

Meanwhile, Mary was having
a very hard time on her ship.
The cruel captain made her
work day and night.

"Any slacking, boy, and I'll flog you!" he snarled, cracking his whip.

13

After a few weeks, Mary's ship
sailed into the warm Caribbean
Sea. Anne and the pirates
were there, too.

"Wake up! Ship ahoy!" yelled Anne.
Jack rubbed his eyes. Then he
raised the skull and crossbones.
"Attack!" he cried.

WILLIAM

Mary's ship fired its guns,
but missed.

When the pirates clambered on board Mary's ship, the captain locked himself in his cabin. "Fight, you cowards!" he yelled.

17

Mary grabbed a cutlass.

"I'll fight!" she cried.

Anne laughed.

"Come on then, cabin boy!"

But Mary fought hard.

"Truce!" gasped Anne.

"Agreed," cried Mary,

"if you take me with you."

The pirates loaded the captain's treasure chests onto their ship.

Mary went with them.

The crew opened the chests. They
found heaps of gold and jewels.
Jack opened a bottle of rum.
"Let's celebrate!" he yelled.

No one noticed that a mighty storm was brewing until …

… huge waves rocked the ship
and rain battered the sails.
The pirates grabbed Anne.

"We know you're a woman," they cried. "This storm's all your fault!" "Throw her overboard and get rid of the bad luck," someone yelled.

Suddenly Mary leapt out,
waving her cutlass.

"I'm a woman too!" she cried.

"And it's lucky we *are* here to sail
this ship because you're all too
drunk to do it!"

When Calico Jack woke up, Anne
and Mary were sailing into port.
"Hurrah!" yelled Mary.
"Let's work together," cried Anne.
"We'll be the best pirates in the
Caribbean."

And for a while, they were!

Put these pictures in the correct order.
Which event do you think is most important?
Now try writing the story in your own words!

Puzzle 2

1. More rum, lads, to celebrate?

2. No one knows this is my wife.

3. I hate this captain.

4. I will sail with my husband.

5. I don't bring bad luck!

6. I'll let you go if you'll take me on your ship.

Choose the correct speech bubbles for the characters above. Can you think of any others? Turn over to find the answers.

Answers

Puzzle 1

The correct order is: 1e, 2b, 3c, 4a, 5f, 6d

Puzzle 2

Mary Read: 3, 6

Anne Bonny: 4, 5

Calico Jack: 1, 2

Look out for more Hopscotch Adventures:

Aladdin and the Lamp
ISBN 978 0 7496 6692 7

Blackbeard the Pirate
ISBN 978 0 7496 6690 3

George and the Dragon
ISBN 978 0 7496 6691 0

Jack the Giant-Killer
ISBN 978 0 7496 6693 4

Beowulf and Grendel
ISBN 978 0 7496 8551 5*
ISBN 978 0 7496 8563 8

Agnes and the Giant
ISBN 978 0 7496 8552 2*
ISBN 978 0 7496 8564 5

The Dragon and the Pudding
ISBN 978 0 7496 8549 2*
ISBN 978 0 7496 8561 4

Finn MacCool and the Giant's Causeway
ISBN 978 0 7496 8550 8*
ISBN 978 0 7496 8562 1

Blackbeard's End
ISBN 978 0 7496 9437 1*
ISBN 978 0 7496 9443 2

Captain Kidd: Pirate Hunter
ISBN 978 0 7496 9439 5*
ISBN 978 0 7496 9445 6

Pirate Jack and the Inca Treasure
ISBN 978 0 7496 9438 8*
ISBN 978 0 7496 9444 9

TALES OF SINBAD THE SAILOR

Sinbad and the Ogre
ISBN 978 0 7496 8559 1*
ISBN 978 0 7496 8571 3

Sinbad and the Whale
ISBN 978 0 7496 8553 9*
ISBN 978 0 7496 8565 2

Sinbad and the Diamond Valley
ISBN 978 0 7496 8554 6*
ISBN 978 0 7496 8566 9

Sinbad and the Monkeys
ISBN 978 0 7496 8560 7*
ISBN 978 0 7496 8572 0

**For more Hopscotch Adventures
and other Hopscotch books, visit:**
www.franklinwatts.co.uk

* hardback